WHERE LOVE REMAINS

AMELIA VANDENBERG

WESTBOW
PRESS®
A DIVISION OF THOMAS NELSON
& ZONDERVAN

This is a work of fiction. All of the characters, names, incidents, organizations, and dialogue in this novel are either the products of the author's imagination or are used fictitiously.

WestBow Press books may be ordered through booksellers or by contacting:

WestBow Press
A Division of Thomas Nelson & Zondervan
1663 Liberty Drive
Bloomington, IN 47403
www.westbowpress.com
844-714-3454

Scripture quotations are from The Passion Translation®. Copyright © 2017, 2018, 2020 by Passion & Fire Ministries, Inc. Used by permission. All rights reserved. ThePassionTranslation.com.

ISBN: 979-8-3850-3237-2 (sc)
ISBN: 979-8-3850-3238-9 (e)

Library of Congress Control Number: 2024918268

Print information available on the last page.

WestBow Press rev. date: 09/10/2024

CONTENTS

PROLOGUE

It was a gorgeous, cloudless day in late July 2017 in Englewood, Colorado. Rachel DeVries had just finished her lunch at a popular upscale restaurant where she and her mother, Evelyn Pitkin, had met to celebrate their birthdays. They were seated with Rachel's husband, Luke, their son, Andrew, and his girlfriend, Miranda, at a large booth, horseshoe shaped and encircled by picture windows, with a magnificent view of the Colorado Rockies.

Seated next to Evelyn was Howard Jensen, her recently hired chauffeur. He had just pulled out a lavish diamond ring from his pocket and presented it to Evelyn for her birthday, after boasting in a forceful voice that it was a birthday gift no one else was giving her! "Mom, I don't know what to say!" Rachel exclaimed. "Did you elope?"

Evelyn had a twinkle in her eyes and smiled broadly. "No, we are not married yet but just got engaged. We're in love and want to be married as soon as possible."

Rachel observed that her other family members at the table looked back at Evelyn and Howard in shock, but then they quickly passed the engagement ring around and nervously offered their congratulations. Andrew began snapping pictures with his smartphone, and the table was abuzz with several conversations at once.

After lunch, Evelyn and Howard visited Rachel and Luke at their newly occupied townhome, a spacious, traditional two-story with high ceilings, cherry hardwood floors, and floor-to-ceiling windows.

"I like your place," Evelyn told Rachel. "It's very cozy."

"Mom, let me give you the nickel tour." Rachel swept her mother upstairs as Luke and Howard made themselves comfortable on the sectional in the living room to watch football reruns. Rachel and her mother sat down on the window seat in Rachel and Luke's bedroom, and Evelyn began to explain why she had decided to tie the knot.

Rachel listened intently, but then she couldn't help but point out a few obvious issues.

"Mom, this would be your fourth husband, and you're eighty-four years old! Are you sure you want to do this? Why can't you just be friends?" Rachel tried to control the shakiness in her voice.

Evelyn had just lost her third husband to a terminal disease two years earlier. Rachel had assisted her mother with her husband's move into a nursing home several months prior to his death. After the funeral, Evelyn had stated emphatically that she would never marry again and planned to ask one of her friends to become her roommate.

Evelyn took Rachel's hand in hers and spoke softly. "What do you do when you're in love? We want to be together all the time, and getting married is the way to do that. I don't like being alone. I need a man in my life."

The two women rejoined Luke and Howard in the living room, where they visited for a while, and Rachel peppered Howard with a barrage of questions with the idea of getting to know him better. The more they talked, the more uneasy Rachel became, and she felt that something was not quite right with the man her mom intended to marry. He was a brawny man, a former rodeo cowboy and big rig truck driver, while her very petite, stylish mother had been a traveling nondenominational evangelist who was always adorned in floor-length gowns whenever she preached and played the piano to her captive audiences.

Rachel wanted to give Howard the benefit of the doubt, but her uneasiness kept persisting, and she could not shake it.

"Don't worry about your mom, Rachel," Howard said sternly. "I'll take good care of her and provide everything she needs."

Rachel looked over at Luke, who had been listening quietly to the conversation, but his expression told her he was not impressed in the least by Howard's boasting.

Evelyn and Howard rose to leave, and after the goodbye hugs were finished, Rachel offered to help Evelyn to Howard's car. Howard followed behind, but his unsteady gait caused him to trip on the second sidewalk step, and he tumbled headfirst onto the pavement. Rachel and Evelyn rushed to his side, but they both knew they wouldn't be able to help him up since he was such a large man. Rachel darted back to her townhome and yelled to Luke as she opened the front door.

"Luke, Luke! Come quick! Howard fell down! You need to help him get back up!"

When Rachel and Luke reached Howard and Evelyn, Howard was already sitting up, and a couple from the neighborhood was there asking what they could do to help. George, the neighbor, and Luke helped Howard to his feet, while Rachel asked if she should call 911. Howard kept insisting he was fine, despite his bloodied nose and scraped arms.

"Are you sure you can drive?" Rachel asked Howard as he sat down in the driver's seat.

"I'll be just fine," he insisted. "I'm tough. I'll get your mom home safely."

Evelyn didn't seem too worried as she slid into the passenger seat next to Howard. She smiled at Rachel and promised to call her once they reached Evelyn's home in northwest Denver.

As Rachel and Luke walked back to their townhome, they looked at each other, shook their heads, and muttered simultaneously, "I don't have a good feeling about this relationship."

CHAPTER ONE

More than eight years earlier on a bleak February morning, Luke DeVries sat at the desk in his corner office at an international telecommunications company in south Denver. The company had merged about eight months earlier with a European firm, and, subsequently, there had been several personnel changes company-wide during that time. He kept thinking, *Why is my boss flying in from Wisconsin today? What else is going to happen at this branch?*

Two hours later, Luke's direct supervisor, Tom Johnston, sat nervously in front of him.

"I don't know how to tell you this, man, other than to get straight to the point," Tom began. "You know the company has undergone a lot of changes over the past several months. Now top management sees the need to thin out all the branches and lay off all middle management. Sorry, man, but we need to let you go, effective immediately." Tom's tone was very matter-of-fact, but his eyes were dark with fear and trepidation.

Luke's face showed disbelief and panic. "Tom, you can't be serious! I put in thirty years with this company! Isn't this age discrimination?"

"I know it looks that way," Tom said. "But here's a list of personnel affected by this layoff, and there are managers of all ages and ethnic backgrounds. Corporate wanted to make it as equitable as possible."

"Equitable?" Luke stood up and paced around his office. "This isn't fair at all. I've given most of my adult life and a lot of blood, sweat, and tears for this company, and you're going to take all that away?" Luke snatched the list from Tom's hand, grabbed his coat, and started to leave.

Tom handed Luke another piece of paper.

"Here's the direct number to human resources so they can assist you with all the exit details. Also, feel free to call me anytime if you just need to vent, Luke."

Luke stormed out of the office and practically ran to his car. Opening the door to his metallic black BMW sedan, he slumped into the driver's seat and dialed his wife's cell phone number.

"Rachel," he said, his voice cracking. "I have bad news. The company let me go."

"What?" Rachel shouted. "Permanently? Or is this a temporary thing? Where are you now?"

"I'm in my car, and it's permanent. I'm going to drive around for a little while, and then I'll come home." He was trying to hold back the sobs he felt welling up in his throat.

"OK, hon. I'll see you soon."

How are we going to make it? Luke thought. *We have a mortgage and two car payments. Who else is going to hire me at my age? What are we going to do?*

He continued to drive aimlessly, still in shock, trying to make sense of what had just happened.

Rachel dropped to the floor in her kitchen and cried out to God, saying, "Lord, I don't understand this! Luke doesn't deserve this—he has worked very hard and has been faithful to his job for many years! We have served You faithfully at church and helped our family during the thirty-four years we have been married. This can't be how it ends!" She sobbed and sobbed for a long time and then prayed, "Lord, You have always protected and taken care of us in the past. I know we need to trust You to get us through the days ahead. Your love and grace will see us through."

When Luke got home, the two embraced and wept in each other's arms until Rachel looked into Luke's piercing blue eyes. Tears ran down into his dark brown mustache and beard as he tousled his sandy-blond hair. Softly, she spoke words of encouragement to him.

He suddenly backed up, sank into the family room sofa, and shouted, "I don't understand how God could do this to me! What did I do wrong? He's supposed to be our loving, caring Father, and I feel like He's deserted me. This is what He allows to happen when I'm only about ten years away from retirement? I'm sorry, Rachel, but I don't think I can trust Him anymore."

Rachel had a sudden realization that the journey ahead was probably going to be long and arduous. She would need to be the one to step up and take the lead in seeking the Lord for guidance and direction for their careers and for the deep and abiding love she and Luke would need to keep their marriage together.

A month later in March, Luke and Rachel's son, Andrew, and Kristy, his second wife of seven months, invited his parents to meet them for dinner at a quaint downtown Denver café. After they were seated at a quiet corner table, Kristy announced they were going to have a baby in October. Luke and Rachel just looked at them in disbelief, because their marriage had been rocky from the beginning, and Kristy had already thrown Andrew out and taken him back just a couple of months prior.

"Here. This is for you," Kristy said proudly as she handed an envelope to Rachel.

Rachel opened the envelope, which revealed a dainty pop-up baby announcement card with a flower garden scene and little butterflies floating above the flowers. The garden was surrounded by a little picket fence, and it reminded her of something she would have seen in a dream of heaven.

"This is one of the prettiest things I've ever seen," Rachel almost whispered. "It takes my breath away."

Luke quickly changed the subject, and the rest of the evening was spent discussing local sports and Luke's recent job loss.

"How's the job hunt going, Dad?" Andrew asked. Kristy's face appeared clouded with disappointment, since they weren't talking about the pregnancy any longer.

"Not very well," Luke admitted. "In this economy, good jobs are scarce, and it seems I'm overqualified for just about everything. Your mom and I are thinking maybe I should use a job placement service. That's probably the only way I'll be able to land a job. Sitting in front of the laptop and going through job boards isn't getting me anywhere."

"Are you still thinking about the possibility of moving to Florida?" Andrew asked.

Luke and Rachel had thought about moving to Florida for years, after having traveled there for vacation many times, taking Andrew with them while he was growing up and even after he had grown up and left home.

"Yes." Luke frowned. "I applied to a hotel safe distribution company in Longwood, Florida, and they interviewed me over the phone. I was one of the top three contenders, but then the company gave the job to a local applicant. It was a really good-paying job too. I'm so bummed I didn't get it."

"I'm sure something will turn up, Dad. You have a lot of talent and experience."

Rachel and Kristy nodded in agreement.

Sixteen months later, in June 2010, Luke was still unemployed and had endured the state unemployment benefits process. He had received six months of severance pay and a modest inheritance from his father, who had passed away shortly before his layoff. He missed his dad a great deal and wished he was still alive to give him advice and direction during this extremely challenging period in his and Rachel's lives.

Rachel ran a small accounting practice from home, and Luke found it a good distraction to help her service her clients. Their schedule was flexible, and they were able to go out to lunch frequently and treat themselves to Tuesday-afternoon discount movies.

One morning, Rachel received a call from Andrew, who sounded panicked. He wondered if she and Luke could drive to Fort Collins, Colorado, where he and Kristy lived, and babysit little Isobel, who now was eight months old, and six-year-old Brittany, Kristy's daughter from her previous marriage.

"Kristy's vomiting constantly, and I need to take her to the hospital right away. Can you and Dad come over and watch the girls while we're gone? There's no one else I can ask to watch them!" Andrew sounded really stressed out.

"I'll talk to your dad, but I'm sure we can figure out a way to get there," Rachel promised.

Rachel and Luke arrived at Andrew's home an hour later to find Kristy doubled over with stomach pain and groaning loudly. Andrew showed them where the diapers, bottles, and baby food were and told them how to get to the local park.

"Put Izzie in the stroller and walk to the park so you can have a little outing. Brittany will help you, and she can also play at the playground there," Andrew said as he led Kristy to the car. "I'll call you this evening to let you know what's going on with Kristy."

Andrew didn't call until late that evening and told Rachel and Luke that the hospital was going to keep Kristy at least overnight so they could perform more testing on her. They hadn't been able to figure out yet what was causing the vomiting. Kristy insisted Andrew stay with her, so Rachel and Luke would need to stay with the girls at least until the next day.

"What?" Luke blurted out. "Kristy is in good hands. Why can't Drew just come back home? Well, we'll just have to take the girls back to our house in Littleton. We still have a business to run."

The next day, Rachel called Andrew to check on Kristy's progress. Brittany had camped out on Luke's den sofa, while baby Isobel slept in her portable crib in Rachel and Luke's bedroom.

"How are the girls doing? Kristy isn't much better," Andrew said. "The doctors want to continue testing her stomach and colon to get to the root of the problem. She still insists I stay by her side. Can you and Dad keep the girls for a couple more days? Brittany's dad can pick her up then, but Dad would need to drive her back to Fort Collins and meet him there."

"The girls are fine, but that's asking a lot!" Rachel snapped. Rachel paused for a moment. "But I suppose we can do that. Dad's not going to be happy about this though."

Over the next couple of days, Luke and Rachel attempted to keep the business going and take care of their granddaughters at the same time. Rachel felt overwhelmed, since she hadn't cared for a baby in a long time, but Brittany proved to be a huge help with her baby sister.

The four of them took walks to the neighborhood school playground, which was empty during summer break. The June air was warm—not too hot—and there was a steady breeze to keep them cool and comfortable.

One afternoon, their next-door neighbor, Leah, invited Brittany over to play with her three daughters. Brittany had a great time, and when Rachel picked her up, Leah said she was a very sweet little girl.

"Thanks for letting Brittany come over." Rachel smiled. "I think it was good for her to play with some kids her own age."

The next morning, Luke drove Brittany all the way back to Fort Collins and met her dad in a store parking lot. But since Kristy was still in the hospital, Luke and Rachel continued to care for Isobel.

After a few more days, Rachel was exhausted. She gave Isobel a bath one evening, watching the baby splash and toss her bath toys onto the bathroom floor. Isobel shrieked when Rachel took her out of the tub and wrapped a towel around her. Rushing to the master bedroom, Rachel laid Isobel down on the bed to dry and dress her in a pink nightgown. But Isobel wouldn't stop crying, and Rachel didn't know how to stop her. She grabbed a cotton swab from her nightstand, put it up to Isobel's nose to clear her nostrils, and called out, "Lord, I don't know what to do to stop Izzie from crying!"

Suddenly, Isobel stopped crying, and peace came over her. Her deep gray eyes peered up at Rachel with an angelic expression on her face. "Thank You, Lord! Only You could have done this!"

After Kristy had been in the hospital for a week, Andrew contacted her parents in Kansas and asked them to come and help take care of the girls. Rachel's accounting practice was suffering from her lack of attention to it, and she and Luke needed a rest. Andrew arranged to pick up Isobel at his grandma Evelyn's house in northwest Denver. As circumstances would have it, Evelyn's sister, Dorothy, was visiting from Indiana with her daughter, Cheryl. The women made a lot of fuss over the baby and took turns holding her, but Isobel would have none of it. Rachel was the only one who could keep her calm, and she laid the baby on her shoulder. Isobel slept soundly there until Andrew and Kristy's father arrived to pick her up.

"Thanks so much for watching the girls, Mom and Dad," Andrew said as he set Isobel into her car seat. "Kristy's parents and I are going to take Brittany and Izzie to see her at the hospital. She's really missing them."

Luke loaded the diaper bag and portable crib into Andrew's truck and patted him on the back. Hugging Andrew, Rachel said, "You're welcome. Izzie and I really bonded, and I'll miss her. I pray that Kristy recovers quickly. Give her our love."

CHAPTER TWO

———— ❧ ————

Rachel had always loved music and began singing in church when she was only three years old. Her dream career, since she had accepted Christ at age fourteen, was to tour the US and overseas, singing and playing gospel music on her violin. But being married at eighteen and having a child at nineteen didn't exactly allow her the time or the opportunity to pursue her dream. Instead, she and Luke had sung in church choirs and ensembles, and she had performed as a vocal soloist and played in the church orchestra. Her most recent endeavor was directing a young women's ensemble called Joyful Sound.

What differentiated Joyful Sound from other gospel vocal groups was that Rachel and the young women dressed up in ball gowns and moved about the platform gracefully as they sang to their orchestral accompaniments. During some performances, a few of the girls danced around the singers in beautifully choreographed ballet movements.

"The pastor's wife wants Joyful Sound to perform four songs at her women's Christmas event this year!" Rachel told Luke as she hung up the phone one afternoon at home.

"That's great," Luke said coolly. "I suppose you want me to help you with the rehearsals." He had a mischievous look on his face.

"I was hoping you would. This is gonna be a lot of work, but I think it should also be really rewarding."

Rachel looked forward to the upcoming event, and since Luke was available, he drove her to rehearsals at church and ran the sound equipment. He turned out to be an excellent music critic, too, advising Rachel on which songs worked the best and which girl was the most appropriate soloist for each one.

The Christmas gala took place in the ballroom of a prominent hotel in the Denver Tech Center. It was lavishly decorated in gold and white with dashes of purple confetti. The backs of the chairs at each table were covered with purple scarves, which each lady in attendance was encouraged to take home as a gift from the pastor's wife.

Joyful Sound's musical and dance performance was a huge success, and several of the women who attended snapped pictures of the ensemble and asked Rachel if they had recorded an album yet.

"No not yet." Rachel beamed. "But we have certainly thought about it. My vision for this group is to record and tour the nation and overseas, sharing our love for Jesus Christ to our audiences and His desire to heal their hearts through our music. We're not just performers dressed up in pretty dresses. We're vessels willing to be used for the glory of God."

Joyful Sound had been ministering in song and dance at various churches, nursing homes, and assisted-living centers in Colorado for nearly five years, the life span of the group. Rachel's mother, Evelyn Pitkin, had invited the group to sing at several of her evangelistic meetings as well. They performed to audiences of all ages; their music was very well received.

"Your songs blessed me so much. Please come back and minster to us again," people would tell Rachel and the girls in the ensemble after every performance.

However, it was too difficult for Joyful Sound to make an album or to go on tour, because the group was comprised of volunteer high school and college aged girls who cycled in and out frequently. Rachel felt that there should be at least a quartet of singers who could consistently maintain the blend she was looking for so she could take the group to the next level.

After one of Joyful Sound's Sunday-morning performances at their home church in Littleton, the father of one of the group's members stopped Rachel in the parking lot and said, "Rachel, I just want to thank you for your dedication to Joyful Sound. My daughter, Brooklyn, has really grown spiritually, and her talent has blossomed during her participation in the ensemble. We pray that your talents and vision for the group will take you far!" With that, he shook her hand and hurried off to gather his family into their car.

I can only hope, Rachel whispered as she drove away.

Just before Christmas, Luke was offered a part-time position with a pharmaceutical compounding company in southeast Denver as its human resources manager. He was also tasked with preparing the whole pharmacy for a move to a better location just down the street from their existing location. It was the first job he had had since his layoff almost two years earlier.

The pharmacy owner and Luke's boss, Dylan Buchanan, a bald man of small stature, also happened to be an existing bookkeeping client of Rachel and Luke's business. Rachel continued to keep Dylan's books from home remotely, while Luke did the banking and processed payroll, in addition to his HR responsibilities.

Once the pharmacy was completely moved to the new location, Dylan took Luke aside, slapped his shoulder, and said, "Luke, thanks for all you did to make this move possible. I couldn't have done it without you."

After that, Luke became more and more aware of how difficult Dylan was to work for. He was very demanding and somewhat of a perfectionist.

"Dylan doesn't value anything I do, honey," Luke said soberly one day when he and Rachel met for lunch at their favorite restaurant. "He criticizes everyone in the office and blows up over little things that aren't important. I'm grateful for the job, but I don't really enjoy it."

"Don't take it personally, Luke. I'm sure he realizes how valuable you are. He's just not good at showing it." Rachel reached over and patted Luke's hand.

Luke pulled his hand back. "Rach, you don't understand! A woman can't really understand how important a job is to a man. My job is where I get my identity; it defines who I am. When I don't have a fulfilling career, I feel like half a person. Dylan promised me at the beginning, in front of the whole staff, that he would make me a full-time employee after a few months. It's been a year, and he hasn't increased my hours or given me a raise."

"Do you want to quit?"

"No, I'll hang in there, but I don't trust the guy." Luke frowned.

"I had really hoped and prayed this was going to work out for you as a new career since you left the telecom company," Rachel said, working up a weak smile. "We'll just need to continue to pray about it."

Rachel continued to work diligently to keep accurate books and meet the IRS and state payroll tax return deadlines for Dylan's pharmacy, while still servicing her other clients. Luke produced a comprehensive employees' manual and hired and fired pharmacists and technicians under Dylan's scrutiny.

When several more months passed, Dylan walked into Luke's office, crossed his arms across his chest, and said, "I've been doing a lot of thinking, and I've decided to make some big changes. I want to bring in one person to do all the administrative work and the accounting in-house. That means I'll have to let both you and Rachel go. I'm giving you three months' notice though. I know this isn't easy for either one of you."

Luke's jaw dropped. *Not again!* he thought. "What did I do wrong?" he asked.

"You didn't do anything wrong. I've been talking to someone who has a lot of experience in office management and bookkeeping. I'd like to have one person do both jobs. I'd like for Rachel to come into the office and train the new girl on how she does the books—if Rachel is willing to do that." With that, Dylan scurried out of the room to bark orders at his technicians.

Cindy Watts, the company's lead pharmacist, slipped inside Luke's office, closing the door behind her.

"What's up?" she asked Luke.

"Dylan's letting me go," he said, shaking his head. "I don't understand this."

"I'm so sorry to hear that, Luke," Cindy said. "Rumor has it he's giving your job to his neighbor, Tonya. She and her husband are good friends of Dylan and his wife. Tonya's out of work, so Dylan was willing to hire her.

"Just so you know," Cindy continued, "I'm leaving the company too, in two weeks. I'm the one who's gotten this company to the level of success it's at, but Dylan isn't giving me any credit for it. I have a doctorate, and I can find a better job elsewhere."

"Wow! I didn't see that coming!" Luke said, shaking his head again. "I think Dylan's going to have a tough time keeping this company going with both of us leaving at the same time." He got up, walked around his desk, and extended his hand to Cindy. "I wish you the best in your job search, Cindy."

"I truly hope things work out for you and Rachel," Cindy said, smiling as she walked out.

"Let's meet Dylan for lunch and discuss this decision with him," Rachel said anxiously when Luke told her the news about his layoff.

"All right, honey, but I don't think it'll help. He seems to have made up his mind," Luke said angrily. "I don't understand why the Lord is allowing this to happen again."

Rachel held him in her arms for a long time, and they both wept. Through her tears, she said, "Let's not panic. The Lord has taken care of us so far. He's not going to stop caring for us now. It won't help to get angry."

Immediately what came into Rachel's mind was, *"My grace is always more than enough for you, and my power finds its full expression through your weakness." So I will celebrate my weaknesses, for when I'm weak, I sense more deeply the mighty power of Christ living in me* (2 Corinthians 12:9 The Passion Translation).

When Dylan couldn't be convinced to keep Luke and Rachel on his staff and Rachel had trained her replacement, she and Luke decided it was time to put their house on the market. It had been three and a half years since Luke's layoff from the telecom company. Their financial reserves had virtually been depleted, and they needed to cut back on monthly expenses.

"Call Jim," Luke said to Rachel when no other job opened up within three months after the deadly blow had been delivered by Dylan Buchanan.

Jim Turner, a Realtor and former accounting client, owned a real estate brokerage firm with his wife, Lillian. He sat down with Luke and Rachel in their dining room to discuss their options.

Jim said, "You could rent your home out, but you need to keep in mind that tenants are not going to take care of your home as well as you have. If you decide to move back in, you'll probably need to soak at least ten grand in it to get it back the way it was. I recommend that you put your home on the market, and we can set the selling price at the top of the market range."

"We need to think about it and get back to you, Jim," Luke said, gazing out the dining room window at the Brandywine crabapple tree he had planted himself. The tree was in full bloom with delicate pink flowers.

"We've lived here for fifteen years, and we really don't want to give the house up unless it becomes absolutely necessary."

Jim said, "If you both agree to sell, just give Lillian a call, and she'll make all the arrangements."

A few weeks went by, and Rachel convinced Luke that it might be best to go ahead with the sale of their home. They put it on the market in early June, thinking it would sell quickly. There were several showings, but the feedback they received from potential buyers and their Realtors was that the home was priced too high.

Lillian Turner recommended lowering the price a few different times, which resulted in more showings. There were a couple of offers, but the selling price and terms didn't meet with Luke and Rachel's approval, so there was no sale.

Lillian was extremely patient with them, even taking the house off the market for several weeks while Rachel attempted to refinance their mortgage in a last-ditch effort to keep it. When the refinance fell through, Lillian put the house back on the market and even held a couple of open houses to pique more interest.

"Sometimes it takes a long time to find just the right buyer," Lillian said confidently. She showed no signs of giving up.

In the meantime, Luke was looking at buying into an automotive tool franchise so he could plan on a steady income and not be concerned about being laid off by an employer. He carefully studied two different companies and rode along with franchisees to see what the business would be like. Rachel provided the financial documents the franchises required. Both the tool companies accepted Luke's application for a franchise, and it looked as if either one would be a good opportunity as a business—in Colorado or Florida. Luke preferred one company over the other since it offered a less expensive out-of-pocket investment.

When Luke inquired of his attorney about the overall solidity of the franchisor, the lawyer stated, "Luke, after looking at the reviews online, et cetera, I don't think it's a very good investment long-term. I think you need to look at everything very closely before you take the leap." Luke remained undecided about franchising for months, weighing the pros and cons over and over in his mind.

Rachel made the franchising opportunity a matter of prayer daily and waited for direction from the Holy Spirit. Besides, she had just decided to dissolve her young women's ensemble, Joyful Sound, since it was summer and three of the four young women in the ensemble were moving out of state to attend college in September. She also wasn't sure if she and Luke would remain in Colorado if the franchise opportunity took them to Florida.

Rachel thought it would be a good idea to have a going-away party for Joyful Sound, so they all met for lunch in early August at their favorite restaurant in Littleton. She gave each of the girls the gift of a delicate angel figurine. "To remember me and each other by," she said.

One of the girls, Camila, stood up and began to cry softly. "I just want to say that I'll miss all of you terribly." Looking at Rachel, she said, "Miss Rachel, I think I'm speaking for all of us when I say that we've all enjoyed our time together, and we appreciate the difference you've made in our lives. We love you!"

Four days later, Andrew called Rachel with panic in his voice.

"Mom! Kristy threw me out again! Can I please come and stay with you and Dad for a few days?"

"Honey, you do know that Dad and I have the house on the market, right? We must keep it spotless and be ready to leave at a moment's notice—in case of showings."

"I understand, Mom. I'm hoping we can work things out in a few days, and then I'll get out of your hair."

"Okay, Drew. Come on over, and you can sleep in the guest bedroom," she said.

Rachel called Luke at the pharmacy, where he was finishing out the last days of his three-month notice from Dylan. "Andrew is coming over tonight," she said.

"Hopefully he doesn't stay long," Luke said with a growl. "I'll need that guest bedroom back in a few days because it doubles as my office at home. The kid needs to work things out with his wife."

"I know, I know," she said, agreeing with him.

CHAPTER THREE

———————— ⧯ ————————

Andrew had worked for a major distribution company for twelve years, starting out as a package handler and being promoted to a specialist in the Technical Support Group as soon as he had graduated with an associate degree from a highly rated vocational school in Denver. From there, he was promoted to a managerial position in the industrial engineering department, but the biggest challenge with the job was that he was working twelve- to fourteen-hour shifts from early afternoon until the early hours of the morning five days a week. Besides, he worked on bodybuilding either before or after work at a twenty-four-hour gym.

His work schedule had been a major reason for the collapse of his first marriage to Daphne, with whom he had two children, Ava and Gavin. Dominic was Daphne's son from her prior marriage to her high school sweetheart. Andrew was the only father Dominic had ever known, so by all rights, Andrew was the father of three children at a very early age. He and Daphne had made frequent visits to Rachel and Luke's home on the weekends, and Rachel and Luke often took their grandchildren on outings to local parks, museums, and kids' clubs.

But after ten years of marriage and their house in foreclosure, Daphne and Andrew mutually agreed to divorce. Daphne had primary custody of the children, since Andrew's work schedule was not conducive to caring for young children during the week. He only saw the children on weekends and holidays, and when Daphne moved with the children to a small mountain town two to three hours away from Denver, Andrew saw the children even less.

Being the only girl, Ava especially missed seeing Andrew. "I just want to spend time with you, Dad—just the two of us," she complained frequently. Every time Andrew heard this, it tore at his heart, and he wrestled with how to come to terms with it.

When Andrew met Kristy two years after his divorce from Daphne, he had hoped he had found a Christian woman who would be a good stepmother to his three children and settle down into a happy, stable, blended family. Kristy wanted the same thing for her daughter, Brittany. Andrew and Kristy were married only five months after their first date. But after a tumultuous four-year marriage, Kristy threw Andrew out for a third time—this time for good.

When it was apparent to Rachel and Luke that Andrew was not going to leave their home anytime soon, especially when Andrew kept bringing in all his clothes and other personal items from his small silver commuter car and stuffing them into the guest closet, Luke said angrily to Rachel, "Why's he bringing in all his stuff? Does he think he's staying here permanently?"

"He has no other place to go, Luke, and we're his parents," she retorted.

"I don't care! He's making his problem our problem, and it's not fair! I'm out of work, and our house is for sale! We don't need this situation on top of everything else!"

With that, Rachel flew out the front door of the home she had loved for more than fifteen years—a stately, colonial, two-story home in Littleton that she and Luke had contracted to build from the ground up. They had selected the carpet, paint colors, cabinetry, countertops, and hardwood flooring. It was built to their taste and style. They had also added a redwood deck that stepped down to a flagstone patio, as well as a stamped, colored concrete path that extended from the front porch to the sidewalk. Luke had maintained the meticulously landscaped lawn so that it was the envy of the entire neighborhood.

There were lovely walking/biking trails in the area, and she (and sometimes Luke) had used them all. On this day, after Luke's outburst, Rachel practically ran to one of her favorite trails, sat down on one of the benches in isolation, and wept before God. She moaned and groaned from deep inside her spirit for what seemed like an eternity, then suddenly grew silent.

Looking up into the beautiful Colorado summer sunset, she cried, "Lord, I feel that this is more than I can handle! Luke lost another job, Andrew has no place to live, my dream of a touring musical group is gone, we're being forced to sell our home, and we're almost broke!" She held her face in her hands and sobbed softly until she heard the still, small voice of the Holy Spirit begin to speak a very familiar scripture to her mind.

He said, "We all experience times of testing, which is normal for every human being. But God will be faithful to you. He will screen and filter the severity, nature, and timing of every test or trial you face so that you can bear it. And each test is an opportunity to trust him more, for along with every trial God has provided for you a way of escape that will bring you out of it victoriously" (1 Corinthians 10:13, TPT)

Rachel was also reminded of 1 Peter 5:7, which says, "Pour out all your worries and stress upon him *and leave them there*, for he always tenderly cares for you" (TPT).

"Thank You, Lord," she prayed. "You are so faithful."

A great peace came over her, and she got up and walked briskly back to the house with a calm assurance in her heart that, even though there would likely be many more challenging days ahead, God still had everything under control.

As the weeks went by, there was more and more interest in Luke and Rachel's house, which was still on the market. One evening, Lillian gave a private showing to one of her clients, who made a very attractive offer on the house.

"This is a very competitive offer, and this buyer is really solid financially," Lillian told Rachel on the phone.

"So are you saying we should accept the offer as is?" Rachel asked.

"I think you should counter on a few minor repair points and see if they accept it. They want to close in early December."

It's already the end of October. We still need to find another place to live, Rachel thought.

Luke and Rachel went on a search, determined to find a rental home that would accommodate them and Andrew, with extra room for Andrew's kids to visit. Luke was thinking it would be only a short-term solution since he was still kicking around the idea of buying into the tool franchise and moving to Florida.

"If you move to Florida, where does that leave me?" Andrew asked one day in desperation. He was turning over most of his monthly paycheck to Kristy for maintenance and child support for Isobel. A biased judge had ruled in Kristy's favor in court for her to stay at home and care for Isobel while Andrew provided their support—even though Kristy was still receiving child support from Brittany's father. Andrew was left with only enough money each month to buy gas, some personal effects, and a few groceries. He would be leaning on Rachel and Luke for his room and board until he was able to get back on his feet again.

After accepting the offer from Lillian's buyer to close escrow on their home in December, Rachel and Luke found a rental property in southeast Denver about twenty miles away. It was a spacious, two-story home with a main-floor study for Rachel's office, a large yard that backed up to open space teeming with mule deer, and enough room so that Andrew could have his own apartment separate from his parents in the well-appointed, finished basement. Besides, the landlord was willing to accept a very short-term lease in case Luke decided to accept a position out of state.

The three of them moved in early December and were pressured to get settled and prepare for Christmas in a very short time. Andrew worked out an arrangement with Kristy to allow Isobel to come to his new home for Christmas, and the four of them tried to make the most of it.

Isobel was only three years old, and she was completely enthralled with the Christmas tree and decorations her dad and grandparents set up in the living room. To Rachel, it was thrilling to see Christmas through the eyes of an innocent child once again. Christmas was a respite for her little family during a very stressful time in their lives—just to forget about everything else for a moment and enjoy the season.

Right after Christmas, the calls started coming in again from the tool companies in Florida.

"Has Luke made a decision yet about our franchising?" one of the recruiters asked Rachel. She was acting as liaison between Luke and the franchisor while Luke worked temporarily for the Denver post office.

"We're still discussing it," Rachel said. "We'll call you tomorrow and give you our final decision."

That night, Rachel and Luke made a list of pros and cons about buying into the tool franchise—either in the Denver area or central Florida. The next morning, they made a three-way call to the commercial tool company recruiter in Sanford, Florida.

After asking several more questions about the franchise, Luke said tentatively, "I'm sorry, but I just think there's too much risk involved in buying into this franchise. I think we're just going to have to back out—at least for the time being."

As soon as they hung up the phone, Rachel burst into tears and shouted, "Now we've missed our chance to move to Florida, Luke! We've wanted to move there for years!" She stormed into her home office, put her hands over her face, and wept.

Luke knocked softly on her office door and stepped in. Pulling her close to him, he said, "I'm sorry, Rach, but I just couldn't go through with it right now. They'll probably still accept us if we try it later."

"No, they won't, Luke. After this, the company will think we have commitment issues. This was our last chance. My mother's prayers for us not to move out of state as long she's alive are being answered!"

Within eighteen months, Luke was hired as a part-time driver by a major international shipping company located in south Denver. The hours allowed him to continue to help Rachel with her accounting practice in the morning, since he didn't need to report to work until mid-afternoon, and he returned home in the late evening. It was hard work, but the company had excellent benefits. And, due to its size, stability and history, Luke felt relatively secure about the improbability of his being laid off again.

Phil Pitkin, Evelyn's husband of thirty years, had not been well for several years. His primary care physician had not been able to correctly diagnose his condition after he passed out at the wheel while driving for work five years earlier. The doctor only treated Phil for hypothyroidism with medication and low oxygen levels by hooking him up to home-delivered oxygen tanks. When he steadily grew worse, Rachel helped Evelyn set up in-home nursing care for him three days a week. She was able to obtain Medicaid approval from the county so Phil and Evelyn wouldn't need to pay for any medical care.

One day, one of the nurses asked Evelyn, "Has Phil ever been diagnosed with Parkinson's disease? He has all the classic symptoms." She recommended Evelyn take Phil to see a geriatric specialist to see if he needed further treatment. Rachel found a highly recommended geriatrician on the west side of Denver and made an appointment for Phil.

A few weeks later, Dr. Jean Lee performed a comprehensive examination of Phil while Evelyn and Rachel sat in the exam room and watched. At this point, Phil had lost most of his motor skills and his short-term memory.

He was stooped over and could barely walk. His left hand was curled and could not open without producing excruciating pain.

At the end of the exam, Dr. Lee said, "I'm going to order more tests, but from what I'm seeing, Phil appears to have Lewy body dementia with Parkinsonism. I'm prescribing some antidepressants, but there isn't much more I can do. He should continue with his oxygen usage; however, there currently is no cure for the disease. I'm so sorry."

Evelyn continued her care of Phil in the evenings and weekends when the nurses and therapists were not in her home—assisting Phil in and out of bed and his favorite chair—until one summer morning when she called Rachel in a panic. "Rachel, honey, can you and Luke come right away? My back went out carrying the breakfast tray downstairs, and I had to lie down. Phil's nurse is here, but she can't stay. I need help with Phil. Please come." She was crying softly.

"We'll come right away, Mom," Rachel promised. "Just take it easy until we get there."

When Rachel and Luke arrived at Evelyn and Phil's townhome, Evelyn was lying down next to Phil in their bed. Phil's nurse was sitting on a chair close by. Rachel rushed to her mother's side and took her hand. "How are you feeling, Mom?"

"My middle back still hurts, but I feel a little better," Evelyn said in a shaky voice. "Phil's nurse has been looking after me."

Joyce, the nurse, took Rachel and Luke aside and said, "Your mom's blood pressure is very high. I think she should go to the hospital and get checked out. I don't want to alarm you, but she could have had a heart attack. Unlike men, who often have pain in their chests and/or left arms, women often have pain in their backs. Why don't you call for an ambulance, and I'll stay here with Phil while you're all at the hospital."

After Evelyn was examined in the hospital ER, the attending physician assured Rachel and Luke that Evelyn did not have a heart attack, but x-rays revealed that an old back injury had been aggravated by too much lifting.

He released her to go back home but recommended bed rest for at least a week.

"Absolutely no more heavy lifting," the doctor stressed.

"Who's going to take care of Phil now?" Evelyn asked Rachel once they arrived back at Evelyn's home, tears streaming down her tired and worried face.

"It's time to move him into a nursing home, at least temporarily, Mom. I'll call the nursing home that Joyce recommended and see if they have any openings." Rachel gave Evelyn a gentle hug before making some calls on her cell phone.

What was supposed to be only a temporary stay for Phil at the skilled nursing facility in nearby Sheridan continued for many weeks to come, since Evelyn realized she couldn't give Phil the type of care he really needed as his condition worsened. Rachel completed all the necessary paperwork and made the arrangements for Medicaid to pay most of the costs for Phil's stay at the nursing home. Fortunately, the staff was kind and supportive, which made it a little easier for her to get through all the red tape.

At the same time, Evelyn's granddaughter Genevieve, the oldest daughter of Tina, Evelyn's younger daughter and Rachel's sister, was going through a complicated separation from her husband. So that she would have a place to live and not leave Evelyn living alone in her townhome, Genevieve came from northeastern Colorado, moved in with her grandmother, and worked odd jobs.

Evelyn visited Phil several times a week and brought him his favorite clothes and candies. They sat together for hours at a time—either in Phil's room or in the cheery and well-lit living room—chatting, reading, and praying. Part of Phil's routine included physical therapy, which seemed to help him get around a little and cheered him up. His attitude remained positive, and he told Evelyn repeatedly, "One day, I'm going to walk out of this place on my own two feet!"

Evelyn admired his faith and resolve to keep going no matter what.

Rachel, Luke, Andrew, and the grandchildren came to see Phil only occasionally, since they had to travel from the opposite side of town through Denver traffic each time they paid him a visit.

At Christmastime, Evelyn participated in the nursing home's holiday events, taking part as Mrs. Claus. Then, once a month, they hired her to hold a short "church service" in their activities room, where she sang, played their spinet piano, and spoke a few words of encouragement to the residents. She was well received and enjoyed reaching out to a group of people who didn't have much to look forward to.

CHAPTER FOUR

───────────── ✺ ─────────────

Two years went by. One pleasant Saturday morning in early May, there was a knock at the front door of the DeVries' rental home. Rachel answered the door to their landlord, Keith Milligan. Rachel handed him the monthly rent check, but the usually friendly, happy-go-lucky Keith looked back at her with a frown this time.

"Rachel, I'm sorry to tell you this, but my wife and I have decided to sell this house. We would like to put it on the market by July 1." He paused.

Rachel was shocked. When she found her voice, she stammered, "Um, I didn't think you guys ever wanted to sell. You liked the idea of the predictable income from tenants."

"We had planned on renting the house to you long-term, but the real estate market is really good right now, and we want to see if we can get a good price for it."

"Uh, can we have more time if we have trouble finding another place to live? We must find a place for two families, basically, since Andrew is still living with us," Rachel said.

Keith managed a weak smile. "Of course, we'll work with you. Just let me know in June how much more time you need if you haven't found anything by then."

Rachel leaned against the front door for a few minutes after Keith drove away. *How am I going to break this news to Luke?* Rachel thought. *Lord, help me.*

Rachel found Luke standing on their master bedroom balcony, which overlooked their driveway and front yard.

"What did Keith want? Is he kicking us out?" Luke said angrily.

"Basically, yes," Rachel answered. "He wants to put the house on the market, and he's just giving us two months' notice. I'll tell Andrew. He still needs to live with us, so we'll need to get something with a finished basement."

"I can't believe this is happening again!" Luke shouted. "Why is God allowing this to happen?" He slumped into the bedroom easy chair and flipped on the TV to distract himself from thinking about what had just occurred.

Rachel said, "I don't know why, hon. It's hard to understand. We still need to trust the Lord though. There's no one else we can trust."

"Right," Luke said sarcastically, shaking his head. "I feel like He's let us down again."

When searching for another rental property, Rachel and Luke found that the rental market was saturated with potential tenants who were willing to pay full price or more for monthly rent and sign two- to three-year leases. Andrew looked online for rental homes as well, and a coworker found a nice, clean ranch-style home for rent only a few miles away from their current home. Rachel and Luke took a tour of the one-story bungalow with a finished basement and made another appointment with the homeowners to return with Andrew. Andrew liked the basement, as there was even a cute bedroom with white French doors where Isobel could sleep during her visits on the weekends.

Andrew and Luke convinced Rachel to cosign a one-year lease with the ranch homeowners and put down a deposit. She did so reluctantly because she felt uneasy in her spirit about the house. This was the same feeling she had had previously about other situations that had not turned out well. Nevertheless, on July 4, the three of them moved in.

Only a week after they moved in and were trying to get settled, Rachel received a call from Evelyn that Phil's nursing home had transported him to the nearest hospital because he had contracted pneumonia, and they had been unable to clear it up. Evelyn told Rachel that Ruby, a longtime friend, dropped in to see her at just the right moment and promised to stay as long as Evelyn needed her.

The doctors at St. Vincent's hospital ran several tests and treated the pneumonia as best they could. They requested Evelyn and her immediate family to meet with the hospital chaplain and the attending physician to discuss Phil's further care. The next day, Rachel and Luke were introduced to a distinguished-looking older man and an attractive, middle-aged woman who referred to themselves as the chaplain and attending physician.

Dr. Karen Morrison said gravely, "We've done all we can do for Phil. We don't expect him to get better. In fact, we're recommending that he be transferred to hospice care. There's a facility right here on the hospital's property. I realize this is a lot to take in, but all of you should consider very seriously making final arrangements."

Evelyn asked, "What about the nursing home Phil was in? Can't he receive hospice care there? He was content there, and I think he'd be more comfortable if he went back there." Her voice sounded strained.

"It's possible for him to receive hospice care at the nursing home, but arrangements would have to be made for a third-party service to provide that," Dr. Morrison said. "It would be easier on Phil just to transfer him to the facility here, where the staff is specifically trained for terminally ill patients. Here's a card with my assistant's contact information. Please call her with questions and let her know if you would like her to arrange for Phil's transfer. If you would like to speak to me again, she can also put your call through to me." With that, she squeezed Evelyn's hand and quickly vanished.

The chaplain stepped up to Evelyn, Rachel, and Luke, offered encouragement, and let them know that he was available whenever they needed to talk.

"Thank you," Rachel said gratefully. "We really appreciate that."

When the chaplain left, Rachel took her mother aside and spoke to her in low tones. "Mom, I know that Phil has been comfortable at the nursing home, but I think we should take the doctor's advice and move him to the hospice facility here. Let Ruby drive you home so you can get some rest, and we'll make a joint decision in the morning."

"Okay," Evelyn agreed. "But wherever we place Phil, it'll just be temporary. He's going to get better. God is going to raise him up."

Early the next morning, Rachel was washing her face when her phone rang. It was Evelyn calling.

"Hi, honey. Last night, Ruby and I discussed Phil's situation and prayed about what we should do next. Ruby convinced me that moving Phil into the on-site hospice facility would be best for him."

"It *is* the best decision, Mom," Rachel said. "I'll call the doctor's assistant to make the arrangements to move him today."

Over the next couple of days, Rachel and Luke drove across town to look in on Phil, who remained unresponsive. They met with Phil's doctors and nurses, along with Evelyn and Ruby. They had so many questions about hospice care, which the medical staff patiently answered. The whole experience seemed surreal to Rachel, since the medical staff made it clear that most patients in hospice care did not recover. They sternly urged the whole family to prepare for the inevitable. The staff's mission was to keep their patients as comfortable as possible during the last days of their lives.

The days turned into weeks, and Phil kept holding onto life. He was not breathing on his own, and there was no IV to provide nourishment to his body. He was wasting away right before his family's eyes. Since Andrew and Genevieve both worked evening shifts, the two cousins met at the hospice center after work to sit with Phil several nights into the early hours of the morning.

One evening at the hospice facility, Andrew pulled Rachel aside with a grave look on his face. "Mom, Genevieve and I have been talking a lot about how Grandma doesn't stay with Phil very much at the hospice center. She seems nonchalant about her husband, who's practically at death's door. We just don't get it." He shook his head.

Rachel thought for a moment and spoke in soft, deliberate tones. "Son, every person deals with grief differently. Grandma has been preparing herself for this moment for a long time. She's spent countless hours and energy caring for Phil, since he's been sick for several years. I think she's praying for the strength to let him go, which perhaps is why Phil is holding onto life longer than the medical staff expected. She's just putting on a brave face."

After Andrew went home, Rachel and Luke sat for a while in the hospice lobby and recounted some of the good memories they had shared with Evelyn and Phil over the years. They had taken summer road trips into the Colorado mountains to fish for trout, hike, and shop at quaint little local stores. They had enjoyed many Sunday dinners together after church, laughing about comical things that had occurred during their family times together.

"Phil has been really good to your mother," Luke said with tears welling up in his eyes.

"Yes, he has," Rachel said softly. "That's what I love most about him."

One weekday afternoon, toward the end of July, one of Phil's nurses called Rachel at her home in southeast Denver. The nurse said, "Rachel, the hospice staff met this morning, and all the staff agrees that it's probably time to remove Phil's life support. Your mother hasn't come in to see Phil yet today, but you and she need to make the final determination."

"Isn't there anything else you can do for him?" Rachel begged as tears began to flow, and she clenched her fists.

"No, I'm afraid not," the nurse said softly. "Phil's condition has worsened, and there's nothing more we can do for him. I'm so sorry."

"I appreciate your compassion for Phil and us," Rachel whispered.

As soon as she hung up the phone, Rachel thought, *How am I going to break this news to Mom?* Slowly, she dialed Evelyn's number.

"Mom, the hospice staff thinks it's time to take Phil off life support," Rachel said gently. "Are you ready to let go?"

Evelyn paused. "I … I think so. I'm still praying for a miracle. He could start breathing on his own once they take him off the machines."

"Yes, he could, Mom. But we need to accept the fact that this may be God's time to take him home. I'll call the nurse back. I'll keep you posted as to what happens."

In less than half an hour after Rachel told Phil's nurse of their decision, she received a call back. The nurse spoke in tones she had been trained to use and said, "I'm very sorry, but Phil passed away only about twenty minutes after we removed his oxygen."

"Was he peaceful?" Rachel asked.

"Yes, he was very peaceful," the nurse assured her.

Rachel called Evelyn immediately. "Phil just passed away, Mom. I … I'm so sorry," she managed between sobs.

"It was his time," Evelyn said, crying softly. "But he's in the arms of Jesus now."

When Rachel, Luke, and Evelyn reached Phil's room at the hospice center an hour later, they embraced and wept in one another's arms.

Then Evelyn, standing at Phil's bedside, leaned over, kissed his forehead, and whispered, "Phil, thank you for thirty-two years of committed marriage. I will love you forever."

CHAPTER FIVE

One evening, a few days after Phil's funeral, Genevieve and Evelyn were preparing dinner in Evelyn's tiny kitchen as rays from the setting sun were pouring into the adjacent dining room. As Genevieve was stirring the spaghetti sauce, Evelyn glanced over at her granddaughter and felt grateful for her company during such a difficult time. Their little Chihuahua-mix puppy and three cats, playing together nearby, provided entertainment and a sense of comfort as well.

A few weeks later, Evelyn's younger daughter and Genevieve's mother, Tina, showed up on Evelyn's doorstep with most of the belongings she had brought with her from Strasburg, Colorado.

"Hey, Mom, I have no place to live since Kurt took back the house," Tina explained as she pushed her long, heavily teased blonde hair out of her face. Tears welled up in her aquatic blue eyes as Evelyn and Genevieve embraced her.

Several years earlier, Kurt, Tina's ex-husband and father of their daughter, Angelica, had purchased a house in Strasburg, Colorado, for Tina, her second daughter, Sophie, and Angelica—with the condition that they all move out when Angelica turned eighteen. Travis, Tina's only son, who had been living with his father in Elizabeth, Colorado, was only two years younger than Genevieve. He had married and moved to Delta, Colorado, several years before.

Soon after Angelica's eighteenth birthday, Kurt put the house on the market and demanded that she and Tina move out. Angelica moved in with a neighbor. Sophie had married and was living nearby in Strasburg.

"You can stay with me as long as you need to," Evelyn promised Tina as she let her in. "Genny and I would love your company."

Tina offered to do some repairs and painting at Evelyn's townhome in exchange for room and board, as well as for cash wages. When Genevieve wasn't at work, she and Tina took Evelyn shopping for furniture and home accessories, and they chatted and giggled as they shopped at the local dollar store. Evelyn felt that she and Tina were reconnecting, since Tina had been estranged from her mother and sister for several years—ever since she had fled to Strasburg with young Angelica.

"Tina has been a huge help to me since I've been widowed. She's been treating me better than she has in years and is very protective of me," Evelyn told Rachel on the phone one day. "Plus, she hired a driver from a limousine company to drive me to and from my evangelistic meetings once or twice a month, since I don't drive anymore. His name is Howard Jensen."

"Just be cautious, Mom. Tina has always had an ulterior motive when she's been nice to you in the past. This time is probably no different. She probably assumes you received a sizeable life insurance payment upon Phil's demise," Rachel warned.

"I think she's changing, Rachel. We've been taking walks and having heart-to-heart discussions about a lot of what has been going on in her life," Evelyn said.

Rachel sighed. "Just the same, I think you should be on your guard. We'll see if Tina truly has had a change of heart or if she's just being nice to get what she wants."

A year went by, and Rachel and Luke went to visit Evelyn at her home to celebrate her birthday. Tina and Genevieve were still living there, and after dinner, Tina and Rachel stole away from the others to the glider on the freshly painted, covered front porch. It was a picturesque, early-August

Colorado evening, with a slight breeze coming from the southwest. Evelyn's petunias and impatiens were in full bloom in the planter boxes, and their sweet aroma filled the air.

"Mom's flowers are so pretty," Rachel said. "She takes really good care of them—just like Grandma always did. Right, sis?"

Tina sighed. "Yes, I suppose so."

"So, what have the three of you been up to lately?" Rachel asked.

"Genny and I have secretly been planning a trip to the Caribbean and Mexico," Tina began.

"We've been saving our money, and Genny is selling her car so we can afford the trip. We want to leave Colorado to live permanently in either Belize or Mexico. I've contacted a nonprofit organization that's training lay people in humanitarian work in rural Mexico. You know that I'm fluent in Spanish, don't you? I learned the language from my ex-boyfriend, Juan, who was from Mexico originally."

"That's right. I remember." Rachel sighed. "But what about Mom? What's she going to do without you and Genny?"

"I've already hinted to Mom that I'm leaving, but I haven't said anything to her about taking Genny with me. Don't tell Mom that Genny is going with me when I leave the country. She'll find out soon enough. Besides, Mom is spending more and more time lately with Howard, her driver. I think she'll be okay after we're gone."

"Tina, I think you're being really insensitive to Mom's feelings!" Rachel shouted as she looked around to see if anyone else was listening. "Howard is not going to take your place! You and Genny are family!" She lowered her voice and said, "She lost her husband of thirty-two years only a year ago!

Rachel opened the front door to go back into the house and snapped, "Please think about what you're doing before running off and leaving Mom alone."

As the months sped by, Evelyn became more and more suspicious of what Tina was plotting and determined that she would not live alone.

None of her friends seemed interested in moving in with her permanently. Evelyn told Rachel repeatedly that when she was alone for a few nights in a row, she felt lonely and a little scared.

She began seeing Howard Jensen, her driver, socially more and more often. He took Evelyn to dinner frequently, invited her to attend a rodeo, and even stopped charging to drive her to her monthly meetings. They sat in Evelyn's living room many evenings and talked about their childhoods, their former spouses, and their children. Howard spun tales of his years as a rodeo cowboy and a semitruck driver.

One evening, Evelyn called Rachel and said excitedly, "Guess what? Howard accepted the Lord as his Savior last night! He read my autobiography and was so moved by my life story that he asked me to show him how to become a Christian. He wasn't brought up in church at all, so this is new to him. The angels are rejoicing now over one sinner that repented!"

"That's wonderful, Mom—really wonderful," Rachel whispered.

One day, early the next spring, Rachel was working at her desk when she received a text from Vickie, one of the landlords of their rental home.

The text read, "We regret to inform you that you have sixty days to evacuate your rental home. We need to take possession of the home again."

Rachel dialed Vickie's number right away. "When we rented the house from you two years ago, you told us emphatically that you had no intention of taking possession of the house again. You just wanted to rent it, as well as your other properties, to fund your retirement someday!" Rachel exclaimed.

"I know, I know, Rachel. But our plans have changed drastically. Our new house is just too much for us to keep up, and our daughters are leaving home. So ... we need to move back into your rental. We need to sell our big home first, so I'm sure we can give you at least sixty days to find another home." Vickie hung up without so much as an apology.

This is why I had an uneasy feeling about this house in the beginning, Rachel thought. *How am I going to break this news to Luke?*

Later that evening, when Rachel broke the news to Luke, he shouted, "We're being forced to move again! Unbelievable! I guess we should've listened to you when you didn't have a good feeling about this house before we moved in."

Rachel's jaw dropped in surprise at his confession.

"Well, at least we don't have to find a place big enough to house Andrew and Isobel this time," Luke continued when he had calmed down a bit. "I think Andrew wants to get out on his own and move in with his girlfriend. Let's talk to him right away."

The next morning, Rachel and Luke caught Andrew coming up the basement stairs on his way to work and explained what their landlords were planning.

"Yeah, Miranda and I have been looking at houses, but I didn't want to leave you guys on the hook for the entire monthly rent," Andrew admitted. "I was waiting until you were ready to move to a place just big enough for the two of you. Do you think you can find something in time?"

"We'll have to. We don't have any choice," Luke said.

A few weeks later, Andrew, Miranda, and Isobel burst through the front door of the bungalow and announced excitedly that the seller of the home they had offered to purchase had accepted their offer. Isobel was ecstatic that she would have her own room painted in purple and a trampoline in the backyard. Miranda was also pleased that there were enough bedrooms so that each of her three children would have a room of their own. Andrew was relieved that he was finally able to settle into a home of his own with the family he loved. Eventually, he was awarded full custody of Isobel, and she was happy and content to be living with her dad and Miranda for most of the year.

Things are finally working out for Andrew, Rachel thought. *I hope and pray that will be the case for Luke and me.*

After a few more weeks of exhaustive searching, Rachel and Luke decided on a two-story townhome rental in Littleton. The landlord was willing to install an additional sink in the master bathroom and make a few repairs at their request. He was also open to allowing them to move into the townhome to meet their deadline.

A little over a month after Rachel and Luke moved into their townhome and Andrew and Miranda (with kids in tow) had moved into their new home, Rachel invited her mother to join her, Luke, Andrew, and Miranda for Sunday brunch to celebrate their birthdays, which were only two days apart.

"I'd like to bring Howard, my driver, with me—if that's okay with all of you, Rachel," Evelyn said. "Since we're going to be on your side of town, we'd like to stop by and see your townhome after lunch. Plus, Howard has a very important announcement he would like to make."

Maria Lucero, along with her husband, Joe, and daughter Deidre, had known Evelyn and Rachel for twenty-five years. Maria had coordinated many of Evelyn's evangelistic services and acted as her administrative and ministry assistant. Maria and Joe first met Evelyn when they attended her ministry training classes and had grown to love and respect her and her husband, Phil, greatly. Deidre assisted Rachel at her accounting firm for two years while she lived in Littleton but quit after that—only because she moved back in with Maria and Joe at their home in Thornton about thirty miles away.

When Evelyn announced her and Howard's engagement to Maria over the phone, Maria was no longer helping Evelyn with the ministry. Maria had bowed out gracefully a few years earlier, as it was taking up a lot of her time, which she needed to spend with her extended family.

"We were going to wait until next spring to get married but decided to move it up to the second Saturday in December, since the church will already be decorated for Christmas and should be very festive," Evelyn excitedly told Maria on the phone. "Maria, do you think you could help serve at the reception?"

"Uh, Sister Evelyn, I had no idea how serious your relationship with Howard was. I need to pray about this before I give you an answer. Is that all right with you?" Maria said rather shakily.

"Of course, Maria. Please let me know as soon as you can."

Maria dialed Rachel's number as soon as she hung up the phone with Evelyn.

"Rach, did you know about your mom's engagement?" Maria asked.

"Unfortunately, yes. Luke and I haven't felt good about my mom's engagement since we first learned about it," Rachel admitted. "There are a lot of practical reasons for Mom not to get married again, but more importantly, we don't feel it's the Lord's will for her to marry Howard. We just can't shake this uneasy feeling. I also turned my mom down when she asked me to sing at her wedding, much to her dismay. What do you feel, Maria?"

Maria cleared her throat. She was trying to choke back the tears. "I love your mom so much, and Joe and I loved Phil too. I just don't feel that this marriage is of God. Rachel, we really need to keep this situation in prayer. I can't even imagine what you must be going through. I love you and will be praying for you. Call me any time if you need anything."

Tina and Genevieve continued planning their trip to the Caribbean and Mexico at the same time Evelyn was planning her wedding. They obtained their passports, sold Genevieve's car, and purchased airline tickets to St. Thomas. They even took their two Chihuahuas to the vet for vaccinations, as they were determined not to leave the dogs behind. They became more and more withdrawn—sometimes argumentative—with Evelyn, keeping most of their plans a secret from her and Howard.

One evening, Howard sat Tina and Genevieve down in Evelyn's living room. In a gruff voice, he said, "I love Evelyn with all my heart and will take good care of her once she becomes my wife, but I hope you won't abandon her and leave just because you know she's taken care of. That would break her heart."

"I'm glad things worked out for you and Mom, Howard, since I'm the one who hired you," Tina snapped. "But what Genny and I do is none of your concern. I know we can't live here after you're married, so now is a good time for us to do what we've always wanted to do—no matter what anybody thinks." With that, Tina stormed off to her room in the basement.

"Sorry, Grandma," Genevieve whispered, with her head lowered, as she passed Evelyn, who was eavesdropping from the kitchen.

CHAPTER SIX

———————— ✺ ————————

"They're gone, Rachel," Evelyn said, sobbing when she called her older daughter the next morning. "Tina and Genny were gone when I got up this morning. I found a note from Genny stuck to her bathroom mirror that said, *Thanks for everything, Grandma. I love you. Genny.* I don't understand why they didn't say goodbye."

"I'm not surprised, Mom. Tina is just thinking of herself right now and how she can run away from responsibility. Maybe she'll learn something by dragging Genny to the Caribbean during the height of one of the worst hurricane seasons in US history. The best thing we can do for them right now is to pray."

"You're right, of course. On one hand, I'm relieved, because they constantly gave me a hard time, but on the other hand, the house is going to be pretty empty until Howard and I get married. Now it's just me and my three kitties."

"Do you think Tina or Genny will call and let you know how they're doing?"

Evelyn tried to put on a brave voice. "I don't know. Tina kept telling me she was going to leave and never come back. In the past, she went for six months without speaking to me when she lived in Strasburg."

"Well, when she runs out of money, she'll be in touch with you again, Mom. It's only a matter of time. Cheer up. The Lord will take care of them and you."

"Thanks, honey. I've always been able to count on you. I've just been hoping you would find it in your heart to support Howard and me in our upcoming wedding. Let me know if you change your mind."

Weeks passed, and as Hurricanes Irma, Jose, Katia, and Lee pelted the Caribbean and US Gulf Coast and Hurricane Maria devastated Puerto Rico, there was still no word from Tina and Genevieve. Undaunted, Evelyn steadily continued preparing for her wedding in early December. She asked her sister, Dorothy, to be her matron of honor, and their only other living sibling, Lydia, decided to accompany Dorothy and travel from Indiana to Colorado to attend the wedding.

All the while, Rachel prayed and cried out to God for her mother, who seemed to want to fill her loneliness by marrying a man she hadn't known for very long and who hadn't been a Christian for more than a few months. One morning, when she was praying for her mother, for Tina, and for Genevieve, she felt impressed to write a letter to Evelyn and express how she was feeling from the depths of her heart:

Dearest Mom,

I thought I would write you a letter because I can express what is in my heart better with the written word than I ever could verbally.

Firstly, I want you to know that I love you with all my heart, and I always will. Although I don't always agree with you, that doesn't minimize the love and devotion I have always felt for you.

Having said that, I want you to know that I still feel uneasy about your engagement and upcoming marriage to Howard. The news came as quite a surprise to us, and I feel that the enemy is trying to drive a wedge between you and your family. It appears that everything is happening too quickly and that there won't be enough time for

Howard to win our family over prior to your wedding. And, as you know, when you marry someone, you don't just marry them but their family as well.

Please be open to how the Lord is leading. I am praying for God's perfect will for you, and I hope that you won't settle for just His permissive will. You are in a very vulnerable state right now, having suddenly been left alone twice in only two years.

Remember that I have always been there to help, support, and comfort you, praying for you every day. I was the one to set up Medicaid, medical assistance, and the nursing home for Phil, as your power of attorney, and I helped coordinate the funeral—not to mention all the help Luke and I have given you in the ministry and at your home. You know you have always been able to trust my judgment in handling your affairs, so please continue to trust me when I advise you to slow down and prayerfully consider these big steps you are planning to take.

As you always tell me, "We have to trust God for everything." Let's heed Proverbs 3:5–6 (NKJV), which says, "Trust in the Lord with all your heart and lean not on your own understanding. In all your ways acknowledge Him and He shall direct your paths," and Matthew 6:33 (NKJV), where it says, "Seek first the kingdom of God and His righteousness and all these things shall be added to you."

Jesus knows all about your loneliness and need for companionship. He has been your husband for several years now and will continue to be throughout eternity. Remember He said, "I will never leave you nor forsake you" (Hebrews 13:5 NKJV). And 1 Peter 5:7 states in the Amplified Version, "Casting all your cares [all your anxieties, all your worries, and all your concerns, once and for all] on Him, for He cares about you [with deepest affection, and watches over you very carefully]."

Mom, I do not want anything or anybody to come between you and me and the bond we have enjoyed as mother and daughter. Right now, my heart is aching, and I feel that there is a chasm between us. Let's not allow this to continue and make sure that our relationship is strong—even though we may not agree with your wedding plans.

Love eternally,
Rachel

Since Evelyn wasn't skilled with computers, Rachel faxed the letter to her as soon as she had finished it; she didn't want any possible delays in its delivery by using the postal system. Then she waited and prayed.

The next day, Evelyn called and said in a very soft tone, "Honey, I read your letter, and I want you to know that I do appreciate all you've done for me. I tell people all the time how I don't know what I would have done without you. I've told Howard repeatedly what a terrific daughter you are." Then she raised her voice a notch. "But I have prayed and prayed and asked God over and over to show me if marrying Howard is not what He wants, and so far, He has not shown me anything wrong with the marriage. Besides, everyone else is supportive of us—except for you, Luke, and Maria."

"We'll talk more about this later, Mom." Rachel sighed. "I think we need to agree to disagree. I love you—no matter what." With that, she hung up and didn't speak to Evelyn again for another two weeks.

The silence between Rachel and Evelyn was difficult for both of them, but they continued to pray for each other several times a day. Rachel often wondered if she and her mother were praying at the same time in the early hours of the morning and how they could pray to the same Jesus but receive different answers.

"Rach," Luke said one evening as they were having dinner, "you need to totally surrender your mom to God. Trying to hold onto her isn't helping you or her. She's always done what she's made up her mind to do, and no one could ever stop her. This time is no different. Plus, I'm still here for you, and we need to keep working on our marriage and not let your mother and her drama come between us."

Rachel knew Luke was right—even though it was difficult to admit it to herself. The only other person who could really understand what she was feeling was Maria, who was proving to be an invaluable friend and confidante. Rachel marveled at how strong and encouraging Maria was during the weeks leading up to Evelyn's wedding date in December. Maria prayed with Rachel on the phone and texted uplifting messages to her several times a week.

"I don't envy you, Rachel, and the position you're in," Maria said one Sunday after services in the church lobby. "You're standing strong in your belief that you're right and that your mom is making a mistake. You two have always been close and on the same side, but this time it's different. I have always loved and supported Sister Evelyn, too, but I'm still holding onto my convictions. We need to leave her in God's hands and trust that He will show her the right path."

"I love you so much, Maria!" Rachel exclaimed. "You just confirmed what Luke told me; I just need to allow the Lord to work this truth into my heart." Rachel hugged Maria and promised to keep in close contact with her.

The following Saturday, Rachel sat at her desk but took a break from her accounting work to write what she was feeling in her journal:

I have been working at my desk almost all afternoon, which I typically do on Saturdays while Luke is at work. It's a beautiful fall day, cooler than normal in the low seventies, and I was only able to enjoy it for two short breaks—once when I went to lunch with Luke before he went to work and once, briefly, when I ran to the post office to mail checks I had printed for one of my clients. I left the windows open all day, as there was no need to run the air-conditioning, and I am doing a lot of thinking … longing for the days when Saturday was a day off for Luke and me to run errands, see family, do something fun.

I also keep looking at a photo of my mom and me that Miranda gave me, which Andrew took when we were at the fancy restaurant for our birthday celebration on July 30. I have two copies of this picture, and I should send one to Mom—perhaps with a card—and reiterate to her how much I love her and miss our long talks …

I like to listen to Christian radio when I am working on my computer, and today Steve Green sang a song he wrote called "Calvary Is the Sea." Some of the words are "No sacrifice I could give to You could match what you've given me. For my everything is but a drop of dew and Calvary is the sea. Calvary is the sea …"

Wow! How beautiful is that? Jesus's finished work on the cross of Calvary is unfathomable! His death and resurrection provide everything we need—for salvation, an eternal home in heaven, healing, peace, joy, wisdom, guidance, and all our material needs. Just as the oceans and seas seem to go on forever, so does Jesus's love and provision for us. I need only to trust Him completely with all my cares, which seem to be just a drop in the sea of His love.

As the weeks passed, the autumn leaves dropped from the maple and pear trees outside of Rachel and Luke's townhome, and the Colorado wind shifted to a biting cold. Rachel continued to pray for her mother, who was busy making her wedding plans and could not be dissuaded from doing otherwise. Evelyn had convinced Andrew to light the candles at the ceremony and to allow Isobel to be the flower girl. Miranda volunteered to find a lovely, long white gown for Isobel, which would match Evelyn's gown. To everyone's surprise, Evelyn had borrowed a full-length white wedding gown and veil from her friend's daughter who lived in Texas. Even at her advanced age, Evelyn was going all out for the big event.

Rachel asked during one of their infrequent phone conversations, "Mom, why don't you and Howard just have a small, simple ceremony with just family and a few friends? You've already had three weddings."

"I'll have to tell you about it sometime, honey. Having a big wedding has special meaning to me. Of course, your aunt Dorothy is coming out from Indiana to be my matron of honor too. She and your aunt Lydia are staying with your cousin Cheryl in Colorado Springs, who will bring them to the rehearsal and ceremony. They're all happy for me."

"I think I need to talk to Cheryl," Rachel told Luke at dinner that evening. "I want to see if she and my aunts are truly on board with my mom's wedding's plans."

"Okay, just let me know what she says. But remember what I said before about letting your mom go." Luke's tone was stern.

After dinner, Rachel picked up her phone and texted her cousin. "Hey, Cheryl, is it okay if I call you tomorrow evening? I need to talk to you about my mom."

"Sure, cuz, call me any time after 6:00. I get home from work about that time," Cheryl shot back.

"So, cuz, how does your mom really feel about being matron of honor at my mom's wedding? What did she think of the letter I faxed to Mom?" Rachel asked Cheryl, who called her from Colorado Springs the next evening. "Mom told me that she read it to your mom over the phone."

"My mother liked your letter and is glad you stood up for what you believe is right. Mother and I both agree that your mom's choices are not ideal," Cheryl began. "But Mother also said that your mom has always been the type who, when she makes up her mind to do something, she always does it, and nobody can change her mind. I know this isn't what you want to hear, but she's going to marry this man."

"Thanks for your honesty, Cheryl, but I told Mom that Luke and I will not be going to the wedding. Maria's not going either. We feel that if we go, then Mom will think we've given in and accept her marriage to Howard. I've talked to the two pastors at our church who are performing the ceremony, and they can see no biblical reason not to marry my mom and Howard, but we'll keep praying for God's will to be done. I'll be in touch and let you know if I change my mind about going to the wedding. Love you, cuz."

"Love you too. I'll keep my cell phone handy," Cheryl promised as she hung up.

One Saturday morning in December, exactly one week before Evelyn's wedding date, Rachel slept in after Luke went to work but woke up suddenly after having a vivid dream. She felt God's presence very strongly and prayed for a long time as she lay in bed. Assuming it had significance, Rachel typed the dream into her computer as soon as she got up.

> Luke and I attended what appeared to be an outdoor event where we had to park our car literally a mile away, and a film was showing, which I believe was a tribute to veterans. It seemed that most of the people there were

bored and started to leave, including Luke. I think I fell asleep through part of the film.

Then it was as if Luke and I and many other people were taken captive by an evil man with blue eyes and unruly hair. I could see the profound influence of Satan on his face. His intention was to keep people drugged or under some spell and then abuse women and babies. I knew I was in danger of being attacked, but Luke was under the same spell as the others and couldn't help me. I kept praying and declaring release for the people who were in this place, which was similar to a commune. Some of them were sitting in chairs against a wall facing me, and I walked in front of them, pointing my finger at them and praying aloud in the Spirit for their deliverance.

I kept trying to tell Luke we needed to get out of that place, but since we had a lot of items we thought we needed to take with us (souvenirs, boxes, knickknacks, etc.) and our car was parked so far away, it wasn't happening. When I prayed with Luke, he would briefly snap out of the stupor he was in, and his countenance would change. But then he would go back under the spell again.

Some of the people there were setting up a sort of picnic meal, and one of the women said that I would be helping with it too. But I would have nothing to do with it. I was just trying to get Luke and me out of the place with the evil man and the zombie people!

I'm not sure what this dream means, but I figured I should write it down while it's still fresh in my mind. I know that we, as believers, have power over the enemy, and prayer and the Word of God are very powerful weapons against him.

Rachel pulled out of her closet a lovely crimson gown she had purchased years before for her performances with her Joyful Sound ensemble, and she dropped it off at the dry cleaner's. She had decided to attend only the reception following her mother's wedding ceremony the next Saturday. She longed to see her two aunts from Indiana and her cousin from Colorado Springs. Her thinking was that she would maintain her disagreement with Evelyn's marriage to Howard by not attending the ceremony but still show her love for her mother and extended family by attending the reception. Luke reluctantly agreed to accompany her to offer her moral support.

Rachel scheduled an appointment with her hair stylist and longtime friend, Lorraine, the day before the wedding. At her hair appointment, Rachel expressed her concerns to Lorraine about her mom's upcoming wedding the next day.

"So you're a signer on your mom's personal checking account?" Lorraine asked. "Maybe you should move the balance in that account to a separate one so Howard can't get to it after they're married tomorrow. That way, at least a portion of her estate is protected for you."

Rachel admitted thoughtfully, "I hadn't really thought of that. If I do anything, it'll have to be right away because the wedding is at eleven o'clock tomorrow morning. Thanks for your opinion. I would appreciate your prayers as I face the event I've been dreading for several months now."

"Of course," Lorraine whispered as she hugged Rachel on her way out.

On her way back home, Rachel stopped and parked outside the bank that held the account she and Evelyn shared. The bank had previously told her on the phone that she could move the funds to a different account without the consent of the other check signer. But she couldn't bring herself to go in. She felt the Holy Spirit prompting her not to touch the funds in her mother's account.

If I move the funds to another account, Mom will become angry with me, she thought. *This could make our strained relationship even more tense. I can't go through with it.*

She left the bank parking lot and drove a short distance to her church parking lot, where Evelyn's rehearsal was about to begin. Luke was not due to come home for two more hours, so she wasn't in a big hurry to get back. Sitting in her car, Rachel prayed and contemplated going inside and trying to stop the rehearsal and subsequent wedding by stating her objections. But once again, she felt restrained by the Holy Spirit to disrupt the rehearsal. She began a series of text messages between herself and Cheryl to keep informed about the rehearsal and the ceremony.

"Cheryl, what's happening with the rehearsal?" Rachel texted.

"Andrew and Isobel are late for the rehearsal, and so are your mom and Howard," Cheryl texted. "My mom, Aunt Lydia, and I have been waiting a while for them. We drove up to Denver from the Springs this afternoon. We're staying at a hotel near the church so we could get here easily for the rehearsal tonight and the wedding tomorrow."

"Thanks, cuz, for keeping in touch with me through all this," Rachel wrote back. "Luke and I will be coming just to the reception tomorrow, so please text me when the ceremony is almost over so we can time our arrival. No matter what you do, don't tell Mom that I'm coming. I want it to be a total surprise."

"Will do, Rach!" Cheryl shot back. "We really look forward to seeing you tomorrow!"

"Lord, give us Your peace right now," Rachel pleaded when she and Luke prayed together that night. "We really need Your strength to get us through the next twenty-four hours."

The next morning at the breakfast table, Luke looked at Rachel with concern on his face and blurted out, "Honey, are you sure you want to go through with this? You don't have to, you know."

Rachel sighed. "I know, but I really feel I should do this for my mom's sake and for the sake of my aunts and cousin."

She got ready, slipped into her dress, and looked at herself in the mirror. Her salon-styled brown hair and brown eyes were intensely set off by the dainty, sequined crimson gown. *I'm making a statement with this dress,* she thought. *The Lord will see me through this.*

As Rachel and Luke were on their way to the church, Cheryl texted Rachel the status of the ceremony.

"The bridal party is moving into the foyer for the reception now. Your mom and Howard are just finishing up the photo shoot in the sanctuary," Cheryl wrote.

She barraged Rachel with photos she had snapped with her phone of Evelyn, Evelyn's sister Dorothy, and Isobel in the bridal room just prior to the ceremony. Isobel was dressed in a full-length, sleeveless white gown with a satin and lace bodice and an empire waist with a satin waistband. The skirt was satin overlaid with tulle, and the back of the gown had a hole cut out in the shape of a heart. Amanda had taken her to a hairdresser, who had styled her ash-blonde hair into an elegant updo with a spiral curl on either side of her cherubic face. Rachel stared in awe at the photo of her youngest granddaughter, already eight years old, and the vision of a fairy-tale princess. Dorothy was wearing a coral-pink satin gown overlaid with sequins and lace and a large bow set off-center at her waist. She had accessorized the dress with a long, double-stranded pearl necklace.

But the photos Rachel gazed at in disbelief were of her eighty-four-year-old mother adorned with the most elaborate wedding gown Rachel had ever seen. The gown was made of taffeta, overlaid with layers of tulle, lace, embroidered flowers, and sequins. The six-foot train had an eight-inch tulle ruffle at the hem. The long sleeves were hugely puffy at the shoulders, with a large satin bow at the elbow of each sleeve. There was an even larger bow on the waist at the back of the gown that resembled a bustle. The knee-length veil was attached to a white and pink silk flower wreath set slightly on the back of her platinum-blonde curls. One of the pictures Cheryl sent showed the pastor talking with Evelyn and Dorothy in the bridal room, and his face showed his astonishment as he beheld Evelyn in all her splendor.

"We'll be there in a few minutes," Rachel wrote to Cheryl. "We'll look for you in the foyer."

Rachel and Luke greeted some of their friends when they arrived at the church and quickly found an empty table at the far end of the foyer. Evelyn, Howard, Dorothy, and Lydia were all seated at the bridal party table in the middle of the room. Cheryl and her husband, Tom, were seated at a nearby table, and it didn't take Cheryl but a few minutes to spot Rachel and Luke across the room. Cheryl motioned to Rachel. Rachel excused herself to Luke, took a deep breath, and glided over to where Cheryl was now standing.

Cheryl grabbed Rachel's hand and exclaimed, "You look exquisite, cuz!" Smiling broadly, she led Rachel up to the bridal party table. The two cousins walked around one end of the table and quietly stepped up behind Evelyn.

"Mom," Rachel said shakily.

Evelyn turned around and shouted, "Rachel! You came!" Rising to her feet, Evelyn and Rachel embraced, and the tears flowed as if floodgates had opened upon them. Howard remained seated but didn't speak a word. The look on his face was one of incredulity.

Rachel then turned around and exclaimed, "Aunt Dorothy and Aunt Lydia!" She grabbed them, Cheryl, and Evelyn, and all five women huddled together and laughed and cried at the same time in what seemed to Rachel was a gigantic wave of total relief. "Thank You, Lord! You got me through this in such an unexpected way," Rachel whispered.

A few minutes later, Cheryl, Tom, Dorothy, and Lydia joined Rachel and Luke at their table, bringing wedding cake and punch with them. In the background, a wedding singer was crooning songs from the big band era, while people at the reception chatted away and ignored his attempts to be noticed. Dorothy made a point of talking to Luke and helping him feel at ease in a rather uncomfortable situation.

"Evelyn asked me four times to be her matron of honor before I consented," Dorothy told Luke. "I didn't particularly agree with her marriage to Howard, but she couldn't even get her best friend or anyone else locally to stand up with her, so I finally agreed to do it. She's my sister, and I love her. I figured I would regret it later if I didn't go through with it."

The conversation shifted to the six of them rehashing old times and laughing until their stomachs hurt. Rachel totally relaxed for the first time in weeks and felt an overwhelming sense of gratitude to the Lord for the way He had orchestrated the whole situation.

CHAPTER SEVEN

———————— ⚬⚬⚬ ————————

Christmas came and went, and Rachel found herself and her accounting practice in the throes of tax season. Tax season always arrived in January for her and Luke, since they were responsible for filing payroll quarterly returns and annual returns, such as W-2s and 1099s. It was an extremely stressful time, and Rachel longed for encouragement from her mother, but she didn't want to bother Evelyn during the honeymoon season of her life.

Months passed without a word from Tina and Genevieve until the next August—exactly a year after they had stolen away to the Caribbean in the middle of the night.

Rachel was on her brisk morning walk at her favorite park in Littleton, passing people walking their dogs, when Evelyn called her on her cell phone.

"Rachel, guess who I just heard from?" Evelyn asked excitedly.

"Was it Tina?" Rachel guessed.

"That's right!" Evelyn exclaimed. "Tina called from Mexico and told me the whole story as to what she and Genny have been doing since they left last year. Of course, they were flat broke and asked me for money so they could get back to the US. They both wanted to know if they could move back in with me and Howard temporarily, until they could work and save enough money to return to Mexico."

Rachel gasped. "I hope you said no to her, Mom."

"Uh, yes, I told her we couldn't give her any more money, and Howard doesn't want anyone to move in with us. We're still adjusting to our new life together. Besides, Howard is angry with Tina because of how she treated me when she lived here before and how she left without saying goodbye."

"Did Tina tell you what she's been doing for the past year?"

"As a matter of fact, she did."

Evelyn began to retell Tina's story to the best of her recollection. Tina and Genevieve had found refuge with a local family in St. Thomas, Virgin Islands, a few days after they landed. They waited out the hurricanes for a few weeks, after which they were able to catch a flight to Belize City, Belize. They found jobs as servers at one of the resorts on the beach.

The two of them enjoyed the gorgeous views in Belize, but they became homesick at Christmas. Tina's favorite holiday was Christmas, and she had always made a point to be home for the holidays. Besides, she and Genny thought their boss at the resort was a real tyrant, so they didn't stay there very long. They had saved up about $10,000 from working, but when they decided to travel to Mexico, they were robbed by the border patrol at Chetumal.

However, Tina had hidden a couple thousand dollars in her shoe, and the border patrol didn't find it. She and Genevieve took a bus to a small, rural town in Mexico and hooked up with the humanitarian organization she had talked about before she left home. They really enjoyed their work there, but when their training was over, they were on their own and soon ran out of money.

"I think that's why she called me, to see if we could help her and Genny get back to the US and give them a place to stay for a while. Howard and I wired her a little money, but that's all we're going to do," Evelyn said.

"Genny's ex-boyfriend, Tyler, called me also, and he told me Genny had called him and asked him for help so she and Tina could get back into the country. He wired them some money, too, and gave them some advice, which he said they weren't accepting very well. Tyler said Tina and Genny were going to enter the US at the Texas border, and as far as he knew, Texas was where they were going to stay." Evelyn sighed deeply.

"Wow, what an adventure those two have been on!" Rachel exclaimed. "Let me know if you hear any more from them, okay?"

"I will, honey. You know, I've been praying for Tina to return to the Lord for over forty years now. She reminds me so much of the prodigal son in scripture. She just keeps running and running from the Lord, but one day she'll run smack-dab into the proverbial brick wall, and she'll have to decide whether to follow Jesus or not."

"Right, Mom," Rachel agreed. "Once Tina and Genny sell out to God, who knows what kind of impact they could make by sharing the gospel with the locals in Mexico if they returned there. Let's keep praying for that."

On a Wednesday morning the following May, Maria texted Rachel, asking how Howard was doing.

"What do you mean?" Rachel texted back.

Maria explained that Howard had fallen the previous Sunday night and was taken to the hospital. He was admitted at the hospital and remained there until Tuesday evening, when he was moved to a rehab center. Maria had only found out about it from Sharon, Evelyn's ministry worker, who texted everyone associated with the ministry about the situation and requested prayer.

Rachel thanked Maria for the information and promised to keep her updated after she talked to Evelyn about the situation.

Rachel called her mother to get the whole scoop. She told her that Howard had gone into the kitchen Sunday night to get some rice pudding from the refrigerator when he turned and fell to the floor. She couldn't get him to his feet, so she called 911. The paramedics checked Howard out and offered to help him into his stair chair, but when he got to the top of the stairs, he was unable to stand, so the paramedics insisted on taking him to the hospital.

"I called Ruby right away, and she agreed to take me and Howard back home, but since the hospital decided to admit Howard, she just brought me home and stayed with me. The doctors said that Howard had an irregular heartbeat, and they were trying to regulate his medication."

"Why didn't you let me know sooner what was going on?" Rachel exclaimed.

"I-I was so overwhelmed with everything," Evelyn stammered. At night, I was so exhausted I didn't want to talk to anyone."

"But, Mom, I'm your daughter! You should let me know when things like this happen. I had to find out secondhand three days later," Rachel said.

"I'm sorry, honey, but Ruby and my other friends have been looking after me. I'd appreciate it if you would just keep us in your prayers."

Rachel felt that her mom had held back from contacting her about Howard's accident because of their somewhat strained relationship. She reasoned that Evelyn thought she might say, "I told you so!" about Howard's health, since it was one of Rachel's concerns before Evelyn and Howard were married.

Rachel started corresponding with Ruby via text, who was giving her the whole story, since she even said herself that Evelyn was only hearing a small percentage of what the doctors were saying. Apparently, Howard had had a traumatic brain injury when he fell, and he was experiencing confusion and memory loss. At the rehab center, they x-rayed Howard and did some blood work, but on Friday, the center transported him to the hospital to perform a CT scan, due to his increased confusion. The hospital did not find any bleeding on the brain, so Rachel believed people's prayers were being answered.

During one of her morning walks, Rachel thought, *I'm sure Mom's been feeling lost without Howard at home, but at least she and Ruby have been eating dinner with him at the rehab center every night. Thank God Ruby has been able to be with Mom, and I hope she can stay until Howard returns home. This whole situation reminds me so much of what we went through with Phil a few years ago ...*

Howard recovered after several weeks of rehabilitation and returned home—just before Evelyn strained her back when putting away heavy groceries. Evelyn had taken care of Howard during his recovery, and suddenly it was Howard's turn to care for her. He took care of the grocery shopping, meal preparation, and laundry. Physical therapists and CNAs came to their home a few times a week to assist both of them with their recovery.

Then, just when Evelyn had almost fully recovered, the local news stations began reporting that a COVID-19 case had been discovered in the northwest section of the United States. Within a couple of weeks, the pandemic had reached Colorado, and the governor issued a stay-at-home order. Almost overnight, most retail businesses and restaurants had either closed or furloughed many of their employees. Office buildings were suddenly vacated as employers mandated that their employees work from home.

At first, Rachel thought, *Oh no, not another layoff and declining business for our company!*

But Luke came home from work one evening and announced, "Honey, my shipping company is considered an essential service, so we're staying open, and there aren't supposed to be any layoffs. In fact, they expect our business to increase, because even more individuals and small businesses are ordering online than they were previously, due to the quarantine."

Rachel also noticed her accounting practice was thriving rather than declining. Her real estate and construction clients were doing well and still needed her services. As the pandemic progressed, she was asked to assist a few of her clients to apply for low-interest, forgivable loans from the federal government. This kept her even busier in the first five months of 2020 than she had ever been. The most difficult part of the isolation was the inability for Rachel and Luke to see Andrew and his family or for them to be able to stop by and assist Evelyn and Howard.

"God is sustaining us through this pandemic," Rachel told Luke one day as they were having breakfast.

Luke nodded in agreement.

Rachel observed a notable change in Luke during the first few months of the statewide isolation order. Rather than becoming discouraged and giving up, he maintained a sense of resolve and exhibited a stronger faith than she had ever seen in him. Luke's attitude toward God seemed to be softening, as Rachel noticed he often got choked up when they read scripture or heard someone's uplifting testimony. They prayed together every day for God's protection and provision, and they saw their prayers being answered consistently. Their church had to close its doors for a few months, just like many of the other churches in the US, but the pastors and musicians continued to conduct weekly services via live streaming, which provided much-needed comfort and encouragement to the congregation and to countless others across the country and overseas.

Then, on a weekday afternoon in autumn 2020, more than three years after Tina and Genevieve had disappeared, Evelyn was relaxing in her sitting room upstairs when she received an unexpected phone call from them.

"Mom, Genny and I are in town and would really like to stop by and see you," Tina said smoothly. "Would that be all right? We can be there in a couple of hours."

"What? Really? I can't believe my ears!" Evelyn exclaimed. She could hardly contain her excitement. "Of course, honey. I'll be waiting for you."

As soon as Evelyn hung up the phone, she found Howard in their living room downstairs, watching television.

"Howard, dear, you'll never guess who I just heard from!" she exclaimed. "Tina and Genevieve are back in town and are coming here to see us!"

Howard looked at her with bewilderment. "Really? Well, I don't want to see them," he grumbled. I don't like how they left without saying goodbye, so I don't have anything to say to them. You can visit with them on the front porch. I'm going to stay inside."

"That's fine, Howard. Do what you feel you need to do. But I really think they have changed. I can hear it in Tina's voice. I'm going to call Rachel and ask her to come over right away too."

With that, Evelyn walked briskly out to her covered front porch, sat down on the swing, and called Rachel from her cell phone. She gave Rachel the news and asked her to come over as soon as she could.

"I'll be there in an hour, Mom!" Rachel exclaimed.

When Tina and Genevieve arrived at Evelyn's townhome, they embraced Evelyn and Rachel, weeping for a long moment. Then, sitting down on Evelyn's porch swing, watching the sunset over the mountains, Tina began to tell the story of what had happened since she had last spoken to Evelyn two years earlier.

"After we talked to you and Tyler a couple of years ago, we took the money Tyler wired to us, paid cash for a beat-up, old car, and crossed the Mexican border at Matamoros into Brownsville, Texas. The town is pretty cool with its historical sites, seaport, and wildlife refuge center. But the poverty rate is high there, so, after waiting tables at a small café for a few months, we drove to Houston. We figured we could get better-paying jobs with good medical benefits there.

"Of course, just like everyone else, we never expected to find ourselves in the middle of a pandemic," Tina continued. "We were servers at an upscale restaurant in Houston but were furloughed when everything shut down in March."

"We didn't know how we were going to survive," Genevieve interjected. "Plus, Mom had been exposed to COVID-19 at work before the shutdown and started to show symptoms.

"Then we had to be quarantined obviously, since we both became sick with the virus," Genevieve continued. "With no income and no way to get food or pay rent, something unexpected happened." She paused and looked over at Tina.

"Apparently, our landlady belonged to an extremely large church in Houston, and she let someone on staff know of our situation. Within a couple of days, they dropped off a box of groceries on our doorstep and continued to do so twice a week for a month. They also settled our back rent and paid one month's rent in advance! We couldn't believe anyone could be so kind to us—especially since they didn't even know us!"

Rachel looked over at Evelyn, and they both smiled and nodded.

Tina said, "We both got very sick with the virus because we already had underlying health issues. But Genny had to be hospitalized, since she was really having a hard time breathing. I was going stark raving mad since I couldn't be with her due to the COVID restrictions. But her nurse kept me updated of her condition by phone and assured me she would take good care of her. They put Genny on a ventilator, and it was touch and go for a while. For the first time in years, I prayed, and I asked God to spare her life. I promised Him that if Genny recovered, I would stop running and serve Him for the rest of my life."

Tina's eyes welled up with tears as she stared at Evelyn's potted pink and white begonias and Dipladenia plants that surrounded them on the porch.

"You know, it wasn't more than twenty-four hours when I got a call from Genny's nurse, Ruth, who said that she was conscious and sitting up," Tina continued.

Genny couldn't contain her excitement and exclaimed, "Yes, when I woke up, my nurse, Ruth, told me how critical I had been and that she had been praying for me through the night! When I realized how close to death I was, I asked her to pray with me so I would be ready to meet God. I repeated a simple prayer after her and accepted Christ as my Savior. I felt such a heavy weight lifted from me. I can't even put into words how marvelous I felt! I was healed from the inside out."

"When I picked Genny up from the hospital a few days later, I couldn't believe how good she looked!" Tina interjected. "She looked healthy and radiant. I knew then and there that God had answered our prayers. I had to admit that God had performed a miracle. It was at that point I determined to keep my promise, and I surrendered my life to Jesus," Tina said as she began to sob.

Caught up in the emotion of the moment, Rachel, her mother, sister, and niece joined hands, weeping and praising God for several minutes.

"This is an answer to my prayers of more than forty years!" Evelyn exclaimed. "God is so good!"

As Tina and Genevieve stood up to leave, they hugged Rachel and Evelyn tightly.

Genny giggled and said, "We've joined the big church in Houston and are working in their Spanish-speaking ministry. In a year, we want to go back to Mexico and work as missionaries this time. Since we speak fluent Spanish and have lived there before, we feel it's God's calling for us. We just came to Denver to see you guys again and give you the good news. We need to drive over to the western slope to check in on my brother Travis, his wife, and their kids. Then we're driving back to Strasburg to surprise my sisters, Sophie and Angelica."

"I wish you didn't have to leave so soon," Evelyn said between sobs. "B-but I don't want to stand in the way of God's call on your lives. This is so amazing. Please, please keep in touch with us this time. I love you with all my heart."

Just as Tina and Genevieve were leaving, Luke pulled up on his way home from work and sat down next to Rachel. "I just saw Tina and Genny driving away. What did I miss?"

Rachel stood up, and she embraced Evelyn once again. Then, turning toward Luke, Rachel beamed and said, "Honey, let's go home, and I'll tell you all about it."

ABOUT THE AUTHOR

Amelia Vandenberg is a writer, vocalist, and entrepreneur. She and her husband have been Christians for many years, and they have served in their local church as deacons, choir members, and Bible teachers. They have also performed on television with a vocal ensemble in Christmas and missions fundraising productions. They enjoy time spent with their extended family and fellowship with other believers.

Printed in the USA
CPSIA information can be obtained
at www.ICGtesting.com
LVHW090034201024
794167LV00002B/353

9 798385 032372